PADDINGTON AT THE TOWER

To Sarah

with love from

Mommy and Papa

Christmas 1987

For older children Michael Bond has
written ten Paddington storybooks,
all illustrated by Peggy Fortnum.

*CIP data may be found at the end of the book.*

# Paddington at the Tower

## MICHAEL BOND & FRED BANBERY

### RANDOM HOUSE
#### New York

First American Edition 1978. Text Copyright © 1975 by Michael Bond.
Illustrations Copyright © 1975 by Fred Banbery and William Collins Sons & Co., Ltd.
All rights reserved under International and Pan-American Copyright Conventions.
Published in the United States by Random House, Inc., New York.
Originally published in Great Britain by William Collins Sons & Co., Ltd., London.
*Manufactured in the United States of America*     3  4  5  6  7  8  9  0

Soon after Paddington went to live at number thirty-two Windsor Gardens, Mr. and Mrs. Brown gave him a basket on wheels.

The Browns' house was near the Portobello Road, where there was a large market, and

every morning Paddington went there to do
his shopping.

After calling at the baker's, where he had a
standing order for buns, he then went on to see
his friend Mr. Gruber, who kept an antique shop.

Paddington liked Mr. Gruber's shop. It was
so full of things it was like Aladdin's cave.

Every day Mr. Gruber made some cocoa and
they had a snack together.

One morning, however, Paddington had a big surprise. When he reached the shop he found Mr. Gruber busy putting up his shutters.

"It's Easter Monday, Mr. Brown," said Mr. Gruber. "And as it's such a nice day I thought I would take

you and Jonathan and Judy on a mystery outing."

Paddington was very excited. He hurried back home to tell the others and then he began making some marmalade sandwiches. He soon had so many he could hardly close the lid of his suitcase.

Later that morning they set off. Mr. Gruber found them a seat right at the front of the bus so that he could point out the interesting sights on the way.

They had been traveling for quite a while

when Jonathan and Judy suddenly let out a cry.

"I know where we're going," said Judy, as
they turned a corner.

"It's the Tower of London!" exclaimed
Jonathan.

Paddington had never been to the Tower of
London before and he was most impressed. It
was much, much bigger than he had pictured.
As they reached the entrance, a man in a

strange uniform stepped forward to take their
tickets.

"That's one of the Beefeaters," whispered
Jonathan. "They look after the Tower."

"They're really Yeomen Warders,"
explained Judy. "But they are called
Beefeaters because in the old days
they used to taste all the royal food
to make sure it was safe to eat."

Paddington raised his hat politely and then opened his suitcase.

"Would you like one of my marmalade sandwiches?" he asked. "I expect it will make a nice change from beef."

15

"A *marmalade sandwich*!" spluttered the Beefeater. He held the object up between his thumb and forefinger and stared at it as if he could hardly believe his eyes.

But when he looked down again Paddington had gone.

After taking a look at the expression on the
man's face, Paddington had picked up his suitcase
and hurried after the others. Several sandwiches
dropped out on the way, but by then he was
much too upset to notice.

Mr. Gruber hastily led them through an arch.
When they were safely around the corner, he
stopped beside a large cage.

"This is where they keep the ravens, Mr.
Brown," he said.

"They've always had ravens here and it's said that if they ever fly away, then the Tower will fall down."

Paddington peered at the empty cage. "Perhaps we'd better go soon, Mr. Gruber," he said anxiously.

Mr. Gruber laughed. "I don't think there's any fear of its happening just yet, Mr. Brown," he said. "That Tower looks very solid to me."

He pointed towards a large black bird standing watching them. "Besides, there's at least one raven keeping an eye on things."

"He looks as if he's got his eye on Paddington," said Judy.

Paddington gave them a hard stare back, but for once it didn't seem to have any effect.

"Perhaps we'd better have our picnic outside by the river," said Judy, when she saw the worried look on Paddington's face. "They won't follow you out there."

But the ravens did follow Paddington, and
by the time they reached the gate there were
so many he'd nearly lost count.

"And where do you think you are going with our ravens, young fellow-me-bear?" asked the Beefeater in charge.

"*He's* not going anywhere with them," said Jonathan and Judy. "*They're* going with him."

"It makes no difference," said the man sternly. "I'm not letting them leave here and risk having the place fall down. That bear will have to stay in the Tower until we've decided what's best."

"Oh, crikey!" groaned Jonathan. "Fancy Paddington being sent to the Tower."

Suddenly Mr. Gruber had an idea. "You know what?" he said excitedly. "I don't think it's Mr. Brown they're after at all. I think it's his sandwiches!"

Paddington gazed at Mr. Gruber in astonishment "My sandwiches!" he exclaimed hotly.

But Mr. Gruber was right. Sure enough, as soon as Paddington opened his suitcase all the ravens gathered round and began pecking at the contents.

"All the years I've been here," said the Beefeater,
"and I never knew ravens like marmalade."

He looked at Paddington with new respect.

"Perhaps you could give me your address, sir.

Then if any of our birds ever get lost we can
send for you.

"We may even be able to find you a special
jar of marmalade to keep by you in case it's
needed in a hurry."

"Trust Paddington to get sent to the Tower and then end up with a jar of marmalade!" exclaimed Judy.

Paddington looked at it happily. "If I'm to be a Marmalade-eater," he announced, "perhaps I'd better test it now—just to make sure!"